Frankie Lov

by Christine L. Villa

illustrated by Kathleen Sue Mallari

~PURPLE COTON CANDY ARTS~

To Lorenzo Miguel Villa

C.L.V.

For CJ and Janjan

K. S. M.

First published in 2017 by Purple Cotton Candy Arts,
Sacramento, California, USA
http://www.christinevilla.com/purple-cotton-candy-arts.html

Printed in the United States of America

ISBN-13: 978-1537628592

Contents

Chapter One

Ladybugs

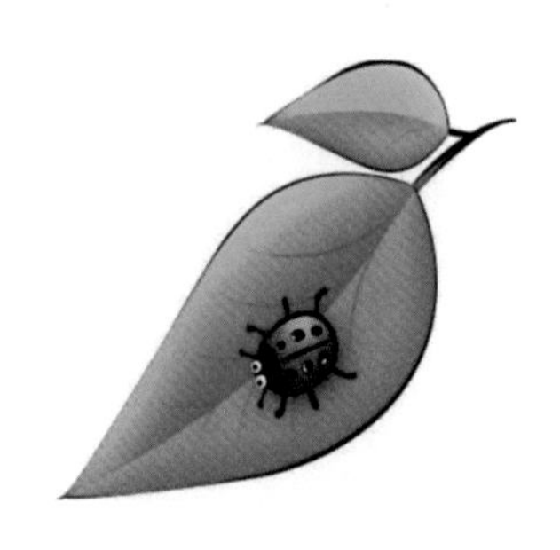

I used to be the only child. Then, suddenly, this teeny-weeny thing came into my froggy life. I always thought that I was the center of the universe.

"How's my cutesy li'l froggy?" asked Mom and Dad.

Argh! Every time I heard them say that, it made me sick. I was forced to say, “Hi, li’l sis!” when what I really wanted to say was, “Hi, you ugly froglet!”

On one very important day in my froggy life, my family and I went out for lunch. Bridget, my ugly froglet sister, came along with us.

She was banging her spoon like crazy, but Mom and Dad thought she was entertaining. To me, she was totally annoying!

After stuffing myself with a broiled ladybug for lunch, I suddenly let out a big, loud, crushing-tin-can-sounding burp.

The gentleman sitting across from our table looked at me and said, “Wow! That’s amazing! How did you do that?”

I was embarrassed and went as red in the face as the ladybug I had just eaten, but it made me smile all the same. It was a feel-good smile because that day I discovered an amazing talent, one that made other people notice me. Especially Mom and Dad.

Mom or Dad didn't say, "Frankie, that's not how a gentleman frog-to-be should act."

Instead, they both laughed and said, "That's incredible!"

The next day, I was excited to show off how incredible I was at burping. Our science teacher, Mr. Bellyfrog, was teaching us a very boring lesson about the life cycle of a snail. When he asked, "Understand, class?"

Everyone in class said, "Yes, Mr. Bellyfrog!"

I, on the other hand, tried to let out a big, loud, crushing-tin-can-sounding burp. A loud fart came out from me instead!

Everybody laughed except for Mr. Bellyfrog.

TOOT!!!

That night, I tossed and turned in bed, thinking of what might be my secret formula for burping. I couldn't remember doing anything unusual. All I did on that very important day of my froggy life was eat broiled lady bugs for the first time. It must be the ladybugs, I concluded.

FLOUR

Chapter Two

More Ladybugs

"Mom, can I have a ladybug omelet for breakfast?" I asked.

"Oh, that's good!" Mom smiled. "I'm glad you're trying something new. I thought you'd never get tired of eating fly omelet."

"Well," I looked at Bridget who was eating a fly omelet and said, "I'm growing up, Mom. And, like you said, trying new things is always good." I gulped down the ladybug omelet and hopped as fast as I could to school.

Ms. Butterfinger was going to teach us a new lesson, "How to Croak Like a Real Frog."

As we began vocalizing, the notes went higher and higher.

"BBUURRPP!" I finally did it!

Ms. Butterfinger stopped playing the piano while everybody's eyes were on me.

"Sensational!" said Ms. Butterfinger. "I'm going to make you the star of our upcoming musical play!"

Everybody loved me!

And so, I had my share of fame and glory because of my sensational crushing-tin-can-sounding burp. I was a hit! The musical play was such a success that Mom and Dad were so proud of me. Even Bridget couldn't stop clapping her little hands.

FRANKIE
THE BURPING
FROG
CLAP!!!
CLAP!!!
CLAP!!!
CLAP!!!
CLAP!!!
CLAP!!!

I also became a famous drum player. I marched, beat my drum, and burped.

Nobody knew that the secret formula of my success was ladybugs. I ate as many ladybugs as I could. The more I ate, the bigger, the louder, the more crushing-tin-can-sounding my burp became.

BBUURRPP!!!

Chapter Three

Too Many Ladybugs

I was enjoying all the attention, when one afternoon, I thought it wasn't fun anymore. While my friends and I were playing hide-and-seek, I was caught hiding inside a man's hat.

"BBUURRPP!!!" I couldn't keep my mouth shut.

When watching a movie in the theater, this happened to me.

"SSSSSSHHHHH!!!" everybody said.

I still burped and burped and burped. Before long, I was thrown out of the theater.

Soon I realized I was having a serious problem. It happened again in class, too.

"BBUURRPP!!!"

"Frankie, cut it out!" yelled Mr. Bellyfrog. "You are disrupting the class! I have had enough of your silly tricks. Go to the principal's office right now!"

I really, really, really didn't want to burp in class. Not once. Not twice. Or three times more.

Mom and Dad grounded me when they found out about it. They both said, "No more ladybug omelets for you!"

I wanted to beg, "Please, pretty please! I need to eat ladybugs. I don't want to lose all the attention."

I was quiet all through dinner and then the burping started once again.

"Mom, my tummy aches. I feel sick," I said.

"What's wrong, Frankie?" asked Daddy.

Bridget was quietly staring at me.

“We should take Frankie to the doctor,” said Mom.

Mom, Dad, and Bridget looked so concerned and horrified. They soon rushed me to the hospital.

“Aha!” said the burpiologist. “Your x-ray shows that you have been eating too many ladybugs. An excess of anything is not good.”

“Have you been eating too many ladybugs, Frankie?” asked Dad.

“I don’t think so,” I answered. I didn’t want to give away my secret, of course!

Mom and Dad stayed up the whole night taking care of me. Bridget kissed me goodnight for the first time before she went to bed. I noticed that she was becoming a cutesy li'l froggy.

I finally realized that I didn't need to eat a lot of ladybugs anymore. I was sure, so sure that I had all the love and attention in my froggy life from Mom, Dad, and Bridget.

Coloring Time

TOOT!!!

BBUURRPP!!!

Made in the USA
Lexington, KY
20 February 2018